W0115536

AIRIELLE VINCENT

I USED TO
KNOW *him*

Copyright 2019 © by Airielle J. Vincent

All rights reserved. This book or any portion thereof may not be reproduced
or used in any manner whatsoever without the express written permission
of the publisher except for the use of brief quotations in a book review.

PRINTED IN THE UNITED STATED OF AMERICA

First Printing, 2019

ISBN 978-1-54395-753-2 (print)
ISBN 978-1-54395-754-9 (eBook)

www.airiellevincent.com

TABLE OF CONTENTS

One

—

AS YOUR OLDEST FRIEND, I'M ALLOWED TO TELL YOU
YOU'RE AN ASS. I write the text and hit send without even thinking.

Earl responds. *Yes you can.*

You're still cute tho. He fires back.

The eye-roll emoji is the only response warranted for his ratchetness.

My name is Roxanne Evans, but everyone calls me Roxie. I live
in North Bergen, New Jersey. I often head home to Rochester Hills,
Michigan, to visit family. And, by often, I mean every other week.
And, by visit family, I mean visit Earl. I had met him over 20 years
ago in middle school. I was the cute third-grader. Earl was the nerdy,
short, and annoying second-grader asking to sit by me during our
lunch period. Growing up, we'd run into each other at high school
parties, sporting events, and even on family vacations. *Yes, so very
random.* We even attended the same university—the University of
Michigan. *Go Blue!*

I fell in love with Earl in high school. He was the star football
player, the varsity basketball captain, book smart, and so very fine!
He stands about 6'2", has beautiful brown skin, striking brown eyes,
and a heart-stopping smile.

Fast forward to now. Earl was supposed to pick me up for dinner
last night, but he conveniently fell asleep. I'm twenty-eight years old

and he's a year behind me, but we're both adults. If he didn't want to go out, a simple text would have sufficed. Clearly, I'm pissed. However, Earl is clueless, unobservant, and not informed of my feelings.

I texted him back anxiously. *You wanna try for tonight, I'd love to see you before I head back to Jersey.*

The three dots appear, and it feels like I'm waiting for an eternity.

I'm heading home from work. Why don't you come thru now.

It's 3:08 p.m.

Unconsciously, I jump up. Take a quick shower. Shave my legs. Throw on some leggings and a lace tank. Then switch to blue jeggings and a cute tank that says "I work out, just kidding, I take naps." After throwing on some earrings and a little pink gloss, I jump on the road.

I text back. *Gotta make a few stops, then I guess I'll stop by.*

I had ZERO stops to make. I just didn't want to sound like I had jumped up to go see him. *Even though I did—don't judge me.*

I make a mental note of the time. I left my house at 3:33 p.m., and I don't want to make it over there until closer to 4 p.m. I start driving slower and weaving through neighborhoods. Earl only lives 15 minutes away, but I don't want it to seem like I'm rushing to see him. *Ugh, this is pathetic.* My hands are sweaty. I'm nervous. My heart is pounding. I'm giddy like I'm still in high school. And my ears are warm. While trying to focus on the road, I'm considering every scenario . . .

I could get over there and we watch a movie or two.

I could get over there and we could just talk, catch up, and chat about our families.

Or we could get there and he could strip me and bend me over the kitchen table.

Any scenario works for me!

Riding through each subdivision brings back so many memories. I grew up down the street from Earl in a subdivision called The Winding Meadows. We were maybe 10 minutes away from each other but separated by a county line, which is why we ended up going to different high schools. That didn't seem to matter; we somehow ended up running into each other anyway.

The summer before my freshman year in high school, my family decided they wanted to partake in a family vacation. It was my mom, my dad, and my little brother Ricky—who's three years younger than me. My mother thought it would be a brilliant idea to go to Cedar Point—an amusement park with a bunch of rollercoasters, games, restaurants, and other activities. I wore a white tank top, blue jean shorts, some white air force ones, and my favorite Tiffany necklace to the park. At that age I just knew I was grown. I'm walking in front of a rollercoaster called the Raptor with Ricky, and guess who runs over and gives me the biggest hug—Earl! Earl, his little brother, James, and I ended up walking from ride to ride together. Earl and I held hands the entire time, and we ended up kissing on all the dark rides, too.

* * *

NOW IT'S 3:48 P.M.

I'm driving down his street and shoot off a text. *Be there in 5.*

Crap bae, I'm not even there yet.

You should have seen the look in my eyes, like no this m***** f***** didn't.

The next text from Earl comes through within seconds. *I'm playin bae—see you in a min.*

I still consider turning around and putting him on the blocked list, but my subconscious leads me straight to his house.

In a daze, I pull in to his driveway, hop out, and head to the front door. Earl lives in a gorgeous three-bedroom, mid-century modern home. When you walk in, the first thing you see is a beautiful spiral staircase covered with a mustard shag carpet. There are three bedrooms and three and a half baths, mahogany hardwood floors, and an airy layout. To the right, you walk into the living room where there's a charming gas fireplace. The entire room is made out of rich exposed brick—which I love. I've been over a few other times to drop Earl off, but I haven't been inside since I was a teenager.

Back then, I'd head over to Earl's house after school a few nights a week—well, when he didn't have a basketball game and I didn't have dance practice. We always managed to have the house to ourselves on these afternoons. Earl's dad worked as a pharmaceutical salesman and would go meet with doctors after Earl and his brother would get home from school.

As his dad was heading out the door for the remainder of the workday, he would always shout, "Stay vertical!" We were both teenagers with raging hormones—did he really think we would stay vertical??? *I'm just kidding—kinda.* We made out all over that house: the basement, kitchen, garage, backyard, etc., but we never made it to his bedroom, and we never took it any further. Earl would always blame it on his coach, saying, "Coach says no sex before a big game." I think he was just scared.

* * *

EARL STILL LIVES IN THE HOME HE GREW UP IN. His little brother is off at college in Texas, and his parents are traveling around the world. *Seriously, they're living their best lives.* He has a long-lost sister, but the family never talks about her. *The story is, she hired* some men to break into the family's house. They ended up stealing all their TVs and a car—which they later crashed. I don't know all the details, but I know it was crazy.

Earl opens the door, looks me up and down, smiles, and says, "Hey."

I immediately melt, but I can't let it show. "Wassup punk," I respond.

He puts his arms around me for a hug. He smells like coconuts and palm trees. I close my eyes, hoping that he can't feel my heart pounding out of my chest. In my head I'm thinking, *"Hi, I love you. Why are you such an ass? Why do you play these damn games? Let's go upstairs now, k thanks."*

Instead, I pull from his arms, push him back, and ask, "How's the fam, scrub?"

He takes a step forward, looks at me, and asks if I really came to talk about the fam. A nervous feeling creeps up my spine, and I'm overcome with anxiety without warning. My confidence is fleeting. I take a few steps back, looking down at the floor and respond, "Ugh, yeah, what else would I have come here for?"

He continues taking steps forward, still looking at me, and responds, "I don't know. You tell me."

At this point, I'm up against the door. He's right in front of me. I can feel his breath on my face. It smells salty but sweet like the kettle corn popcorn we used to buy at the Michigan football games. I'm trying desperately not to look up, not to look at his face, not look into his gorgeous eyes. I don't respond, and I manage not to look up. I'm frozen.

I'm sure thousands of women have been stuck in this same place hundreds of times. Earl has this way of making you feel safe, sexy, and wanted. In college, I'd always see him sitting around flirting with the ladies at The Union—our university's hangout spot. I wasn't then, nor am I now, the kind of woman who wants to flirt just to flirt. I want to know it's going to lead to more. Otherwise, what's the point? Earl knew my feelings on the topic. For the most part, he was respectful of them.

Shortly after Earl graduated from college, he did trick me into thinking he had gotten his shit together. He sent me a long message about how he missed me and wanted to talk about taking our relationship to the next step. I should have known he was up to no good, since the text came through at 10:59 p.m. My grandma always told me there's nothing open that late except fast food restaurants and strippers. Earl asked me to come talk. We ended up not talking at all.

After responding to his text that night, I rolled outta bed. It was shortly after 11 p.m.—on a Friday night, mind you—that I was headed to his house. We started the evening out on his bed watching the movie *Norbit*. We were half watching and half trying to nonchalantly rip off each other's clothing. He's always done this thing that drives me insane—he grabs my face and kisses me in a way that makes me feel like there's no one else in the world. Unfortunately, that night ended abruptly when his then girlfriend—who I had no idea about—ended up crashing the party. Clearly, he was lying about what he wanted to talk to me about, and it was doubtful he actually intended to have a conversation with me at all. Needless to say, Earl and I didn't talk for a few years after that.

* * *

I SNAP BACK TO MY DAZE, BUT I'M ALMOST WISHING I HADN'T, AS NOW I HAVE THESE UNRESOLVED FEELINGS OF ANGER AND DISAPPOINTMENT THAT WEREN'T THERE A MINUTE AGO. Earl takes one look at my face and starts apologizing, though it's clear he's confused as to why I'm pissed. However, to me, it makes complete sense. He's been playing this yo-yo game with me for over 20 years. He takes me for granted—only reaching out to me when he wants me and/or when it's convenient for him. I'm the idiot that keeps going back for more, though.

Earl takes his hand and lifts my face to look at his. "I'm sorry bae, don't be mad at me," he responds to the look on my face.

"I'm not. I don't care," I say back quickly with a scowl.

"You don't care?" he says, moving his left hand to my waist, slowly sliding it under my shirt.

"Why would I care so much about someone who doesn't care about me?" I snap back, trying to concentrate on my rebuttals instead of his hand moving along the waist of my jeans.

"Shut up," he says.

I look up pissed AF, and he leans down to kiss me. I push him back, but he takes a step closer. He pushes me against the door, grabs both of my hands, and pins them together above my head. I shudder as he kisses my lips.

He whispers, "You don't care." It is said in a teasing way, because at the same time, he is moving his hands from above my head, to my waist, then to my breasts. My eyes are closed, my vagina is pulsing, my breath is slow, and it's like my body has a mind of its own.

I wrestle my hands away from his grip, putting them in the air, giving him the freedom to start taking my clothes off. Earl slides off my top, revealing a black and red lace bra. He stares at me for a second—clearly my marathon training has been paying off. *YAY! Self-high-five!* Without saying another word, he grabs my hand, and leads me upstairs to his room.

The master bedroom is black and brown with turquoise accents. From the door, the first thing you see is the bed. It's a king—maybe a California king—and the entire headboard is a mirror. The sheets and bedspread are jet-black. To the right, there's a long, brown dresser that takes up most of the wall. On top of it, there's another mirror staring right at me. I look away after seeing myself half-naked, awkwardly standing in the doorway. There is a brown nightstand on each side of the bed, and a bright turquoise love seat to the left. I've always wondered what's the point of having a couch and a bed in the same room, but I guess some people think it looks good. After taking in the sights, I realize I'm shivering. It's freezing, and the blackout shades are blocking out any hope of warmth or sunlight. The only glimmer of light is seeping in the room from the hallway.

"What is it that you want?" I ask from the door.

"Well, first, I want you to come here," he pats the bed and motions me to sit next to him.

Without hesitation I walk over and sit, like I'm under a spell. "Hi," I whisper.

"Hi back," he responds. I lean my face in closer to his. He gives me a peck. Quickly he stands up, puts his hands on both sides of my hips, and slides me back on the bed with ease. I watch in awe as he pulls his shirt over his head, revealing a gray wife beater and a dog tag with his name on it. Earl has strong arms, a broad chest, and nice abs. *That I'd love to lick at this moment.* I sit up to try to pull off his pants, but he pushes me back. He slides off his jeans and pulls off my jeggings in a few quick motions.

Before climbing out of the bed, Earl grabs something out of the drawer next to his dresser. I start to ask what it is, but before I know it, he's in between my legs, moving my thong to the side and kissing, then sucking, on my sweet spot. I grab a pillow to put over my face but he pulls it from me and throws it on the floor. He moves from my clit to my stomach, to my neck, whispering, "You still don't care."

He then slides two fingers inside of me, his thumb rubbing around that same spot, sending *my eyes to the back of my head.* From under him, I awkwardly pull my thong off, inching it down to my toes.

"Kiss me," I respond. His sweet and salty tongue licks the top of my lip before sliding in my mouth. He's wrapped in between my legs, his dick pushing against my lower stomach. "Put it in," I request between kisses.

As I look up at him now, he seems much more mature—clearly because we're no longer teenagers. Earl is the lead project engineer for a major technology company. He drives a brand-new Infinity Q50 and probably has multiple women. Yet, I'm still here almost naked, lying in his bed.

Earl slides off his shorts, puts on a condom, and thrusts inside of me. It's a tad bit uncomfortable, but nothing I can't handle. "You are mine," he lets out while grinding against me. "All mine," he swears again, pinning my hands above my head. My eyes are closed, and my breath is heavy. Every time he put his tongue in my mouth I suck it—as if I were sucking his dick—making his penis get just a little harder inside of me.

It's been a while for me, so every pump brings out a moan, sending me closer and closer to cumming. "You still don't care," he jokes.

I grab his face and slide my tongue inside his mouth. "Harder," is the only response that comes out of my mouth.

In an instant, he stands me up, turns me around, and pushes me forward. My feet are on the floor, and my elbows are pressing into the bed. One of his hands is pushing against my back, the other grabbing my ass. After a few quick thrusts, he uses his foot to move my right foot farther to the right, so I'm lower and he can go deeper inside of me. My breasts are bouncing uncontrollably, and the mirror in front of the bed is giving me a full view of my slutdom.

"Baby," he whispers, "I'm not gonna last like this."

Not ready for it to end, I push back, motioning for him to get onto the bed. "Move," I demand.

I slowly sit on his dick, moving up and down, timing the thrusts with my breaths. The more I get into it, the faster I go. Earl wraps his arms around my waist and pushes farther into me. Before I know it, he is reaching behind me, sliding off my bra on the first try.

He makes a sucking noise on my left nipple, and my toes curl. As I ride his dick, he's slowly licking around my breast, giving soft kisses, while his other hand grips my ass. The rougher he gets, the faster I move. I lean over, saying "I want every inch of your dick inside me." He grabs my face, putting his entire tongue in the back of my throat. Kissing him, while fucking him, makes me wetter. My breathing gets harder as he grips my ass, whispering for me to cum on his dick. I try to resist, but it's impossible. Every point in my body sparks with desire; my back arches, my mouth drops, and I lose all control of my senses.

"Flip over," he says, flipping me on my stomach, away from the mirror. He slides his dick back inside of me and positions my hips so that I'm up on all fours.

He's giving me quick but hard pumps, and the more he slides inside of me, the louder I get. "Fuck me!" I'm now shouting. His hands grip my waist tighter than before; he holds his dick inside of me for a few moments, then collapses back onto the bed.

It's over. My mind is racing. *Damn, is that what I've been missing out on for the last 20-somethin' years?* Then shock and panic ensue. *OMG, what did I just do? What's going to happen next? Should I just leave—and OMG, where are my clothes???*

My back is to the wall, I'm frozen with fear, and then I decide to make a beeline to the door. Half my clothes are downstairs, so I decide that I'll grab some shorts from the laundry room and just take off—and we'll act like this never happened.

I move my right foot to start my exit, but he grabs me and pulls me backwards. "Where do you think you're going?" he asks.

I don't answer. He pulls me close so my back is against his rock-hard abs. He wraps his arms around me, kissing my neck. "Don't go anywhere, okay," he says.

Frozen again, I respond, "Okay, baby."

* * *

BANG, BANG, BANG. Someone's knocking on my car window.

"Roxie!" Earl says. I quickly snap out of my daze, realizing it was all just a daydream. "I'm so sorry about last night. Come on in; I got us some sushi."

Two

—

5 a.m. Alarm goes off.

Hit snooze.

5:10 a.m. Second alarm goes off.

5:12 a.m. Roll out of bed and throw on gym clothes.

Drive to the gym.

5:30 a.m. Five-mile run on the treadmill.

6:30 a.m. Shower, get dressed, and head into work.

It's Monday. Again. #thestruggle

I should be logging on. Checking emails. Returning voicemails. Making my task list for the day. The only thing on my mind is the epic fail of a weekend I had with Earl. I'm obviously madly in love with someone who just wants to sit at the kitchen table, eat sushi, and reminisce about the old days.

Last evening after I snapped out of my daze, we ended up chatting about college football and the family just like every other time we've hung out since our awkward "*Norbit* night." I'm starting to wonder why I'm spending so much money taking trips home to see someone I could chat with on Facetime. In the beginning, I thought Earl was playing hard to get. Now, I'm actually starting to think he's just not that into me.

I'm almost 30, still single, going on pointless trips home, and I'm not getting any closer to finding love.

"Roxie!" my manager, Max, yells at me. "Are you here with us today?"

He has caught me staring out the window, AGAIN. Max is a tiny, Chaldean, middle-aged man with a wife and family. By tiny, I mean he's 5'1" and about 120 pounds. He wears the same type outfit every day—a button-up shirt and tie with matching socks. He switches back and forth from corduroy pants to slim boot cut jeans.

I'm currently employed as a purchase banker at Excel Loans. I really have a passion for television news, but that job is almost impossible to break into unless you know someone—which I don't. This is what I do to pay the bills, including those student loans that continue to pile up.

My job is to make sure people are qualified to buy a home. I ask about their income, current situation, and how much they have in the bank. I insert their information into a program and then, magically, I can tell people if they are eligible for their dream home, if they should look for a shack, or if they should stay in their mama's basement.

As a 28-year-old English major dreaming of a career in TV news, am I qualified to make these decisions? Well, I've gone through a rigorous two-month training, I've passed at least five certification exams, and my boss tells me I'm brilliant. But fuck no. I'm not qualified for this shit.

There was this one time that I was working with a woman who wanted to move from California to Maine. I told this woman she was qualified to move into a $250,000 home. On my word—and my company's approval—she packed up her home and started driving a U-Haul in a truck across the country. Of course, it's not that easy. There are underwriters who check my work. My manager checks my work. There are tons of checks and balances. Somehow, though, this loan made it through the cracks. At the closing table, someone told this sweet 63-year-old woman that I had missed her student loans—from ages ago—and now that we've seen them, she's no longer qualified. I'm pretty sure I should have been fired for that. However, three and a half years later, I'm still helping people find their forever homes.

As I was saying, I'm probably not qualified to make such a big decision in someone's life. But here I am. Doing it every day.

My phone starts ringing. It's one of my nosey clients who loves to stalk me on Facebook and talk about my current single status. Ryan Rubble is the sweetest gay man I've ever spoken with. He works in the marketing department at Disney and makes well over six figures. Right now, he's buying the perfect dream home for his husband and their adopted son.

"Roxie, Roxie, Roxie," he says to me. "We have got to get you a man."

No shit. "I'm a strong, black, independent woman, Mr. Rubble, I'm fine," I fire back.

He starts laughing uncontrollably.

"We can't all find our perfect man at Disney when we're 25 years old and spend the rest of our lives living happily ever after," I respond.

"Did I tell you we met at Disney, honey? We met on Tinder. Ggggiiiirrrrllll, he spent one fiery night with me and has been following me around ever since."

I pause to think about online dating. My grandma bought me a three-month subscription to Match.com for Christmas, and my mother has been trying to get me to try it out ever since. Online dating is just so weird. Why can't I just run into a guy at the library and we instantly fall madly in love with each other?

"Roxie, you there?" Ryan asks.

"Yes, I'm sorry. The reason I asked you to call is because we need your bank statements. Can you fax or email them over to me?" I ask.

"Sending them over now, boo. Walking into a meeting. Don't forget to check out Tinder. Ciao, Bella."

Me on Tinder. *Nope.* Not going to happen. Not now, not ever. I know I'll meet someone, somewhere. Maybe it will happen at the library or perhaps the gym. Or even on tonight's venture to the grocery store.

After work, I head to Kroger because I have absolutely NOTHING in my fridge at home. Instead of making a list like normal, I decide to wing it. How bad could it be?

I make it to the checkout line, and I have everything from Oreo cookies to hummus and veggies to frozen vegetarian meals to water bottles by the dozen. Call me old-fashioned, but I prefer to actually get in line and chat with the employees while they ring me up instead of heading to the self-checkout line.

While I'm loading my items onto the conveyor belt, a man gets in line behind me. He's about six feet tall and extremely handsome. He looks to be of Italian descent with gorgeous green eyes. He's wearing the new Hoka running shoes—which is a major plus because that means he takes care of his feet. He also has on gym clothes—which means he works out. I'm in front of the cart, removing all the little items, and he starts grabbing some of the heavy items at the bottom of the cart for me.

"Thank you so much," I say as I look up into his beautiful green eyes and know that he is the love of my life and that we will spend forever together.

"No problem," he says back, confirming the *raging passion* he has for me. I know we both feel the spark, but before I can get another word out, the woman checking me out asks, "Those cucumbers—are they yours or his? Or are you guys together?"

"Not yet," flies out of my mouth with an awkward laugh. It's like I'm in a movie and I can see the words slowly flying out of my mouth.

"The cucumbers are mine," my future husband says, politely grabbing them and his tortilla chips. He then backs away and sprints for the self-checkout lane.

The lady checking me out says, "Maybe next time."

Completely embarrassed, I grab my bags and briskly walk to the car. My face is hot, my armpits are sweating, and my embarrassment is at an all-time high. I throw the bags in the trunk, pull out my phone, download Tinder, and throw my phone on the passenger seat.

I have a silent ride home.

* * *

THAT NIGHT IN BED, I MAKE A TINDER ACCOUNT THROUGH MY FACEBOOK PAGE. On the app, you swipe left if you're not interested. You swipe right if you think the person is attractive and want to get to know them. If they swipe right on you as well, then you are paired up as a match. That means you can start chatting with each other and see if you want to take it further.

With my head propped up on several pillows, I swipe left A LOT. However, I find a few people attractive and start getting matches almost immediately.

One guy really catches my eye—a Michael W. Forrester. That sounds like a strong intelligent black man, right? I start going through his pictures, and the second photo I see is a picture of him and his mama. *Awkward, am I right?* Still, it doesn't go off as a red flag in my head. He's a light-skinned African-American man with hazel eyes. I can't tell how tall he is from the pictures, but they do show me that he runs track—the 400 hurdles, to be exact.

Feeling daring, I send off a message: "Hey."

A day goes by, and I go into the app to check for responses. There is nothing. Pissed off, I double tap the home button on my iPhone and close the app. The nerve. This fool swiped right, matched with me, and is not answering my message.

Another day goes by, no answer.

Day three rolls around, I open the app to delete my profile, and there's one unread message. I open it. It's a GIF of a bear, waving hello.

Really bro, that's the best you could do. Annoyed, I send back a middle finger. Fuck it. I'm getting off the app anyway.

He sends back, "LOL. My kind of girl."

I fire back, "Maybe you would have gotten a better response if you didn't take damn near a week to respond."

He writes, "I didn't know I was on a time limit."

Ugh. I hate smartasses.

A few hours go by. "Your pictures are cute, I'd love to meet you."

"I don't really care to meet you," I respond.

"Damn, that's real," he types.

"What did you have in mind?" I write back, feeling bad about my last message.

"Why don't you come over to my place?" he says.

Um, what the fuck does he think this is? "Nah, I'm good fam. Thanks though," I fire back. *The fastest way to piss somebody off is by calling them 'fam.'*

"Well, if you change your mind, here's my address," he writes, including his address in all caps. "Come by around 8 p.m. tonight."

As someone who is clearly brand-new to this online dating idea, I'm shocked. Do people really do this? Just go meet someone in person that they randomly meet on Tinder? I'm not going to do this. There's no way. I'm not that thirsty.

* * *

7:00 p.m. Jumped in the shower

7:15 p.m. Stared at the messages some more

7:30 p.m. In the car, inputting his address into my phone

7:35 p.m. Fired off a text. *Be there in a bit.*

7:36 p.m. Michael responds. *K.*

The entire drive over to Michael's, I'm trying to decide if I'm really going to go through with it. I'm wearing a tank top with a Nike hoodie over it that says "Just Do It," black leggings, and black Puma gym shoes. I wanted to dress comfy just in case I have to jump up and kick someone's ass or run.

Michael's apartment complex looks like a low-security prison. When you pull in from the main road, there are black fences with barbed wire at the top surrounding the complex. From the back of the line of cars, I can see six long, white-brick buildings that appear to be falling apart. As I inch closer to the gate, more and more sketchy details become visible.

The six buildings are laid out in a row, separated by parking lots. In the lot directly in front of me, there are two cop cars with their lights flashing. I'm not sure what's going on, and I really don't want to find out. Driving in, behind the gates, doesn't make me feel any safer. My GPS tells me to drive straight back, then take a right. While passing building number three, I see a man—whom I assume is drunk—passed out in the grass. I also pass multiple cars with people smoking—what I assume is marijuana—inside. My immediate reaction is to lock the doors. I feel nervous, not only because I'm meeting a guy I just met on Tinder, but also because my safety is probably in jeopardy. My heart is in my throat, and I'm hoping the last three minutes of this drive go by quickly.

Michael lives in the last building on the right. While driving farther back, I see cups and trash littering the grassy area of the community. And there's a terrible smell permeating through my window. It smells like something died.

DING. My car alerts me to a new text message, then reads it out aloud. "Where you at?" Michael sends.

I pull up to his apartment building, and the first thing I see is the dumpster. I guess that's to blame for the terrible smell. There's also a man sitting outside staring at his cell phone. He's about 15 feet away and wearing black pants, a black hoodie covering his face, and there's a pit bull sitting next to him who's off the leash.

"I'm here," I send back. "In the white jeep."

The man in the black hoodie stands up and starts walking toward my car. I open the door, but before I can say anything, the pit bull starts charging at me. "Ice!" the man yells, but that has zero effect on the dog. I probably should have been scared, but I have a 100-pound dog at home, and my parents have a pit bull, so that emotion never crossed my mind. I crouch down right before the dog gets to my feet.

"She's a vicious killer, you don't want to do that," the man says. Instead of ferociousness, I'm met with lots of wet kisses and a soft whimper of love.

"I'm just playing, she's a big baby," the mysterious man says.

"You should really have her on a leash out here," I fire back.

"For what?" he asks.

"Number one because pit bulls are illegal breeds and number two because someone could hurt her," I say, pissed off at his stupid response.

The man puts his hand out, "I'm Michael."

"Roxie," I fire back, still annoyed.

"You comin' in?" he asks, making a motion toward the door.

"I haven't decided yet," I respond, still playing with the gorgeous puppy. Ice is about 60 pounds. She's gray with white paws and a white heart on her nose. I'm absolutely in love.

Before Michael can get out another smart-ass comment, I declare, "I'll come in for her, but that's the only thing keeping me here."

"For now," he quietly murmurs while turning away and leading me to his apartment. After he turns around and I'm positive he can't see me, I crack a smile. I love a clever man.

Michael looks much different in person than he does in his picture. He's about 6"0' and thin. His hair is not cut, and he has a scruffy beard. But there's something about him that makes me feel safe—or maybe it's the puppy; I can't tell.

We walk into Michael's apartment, and it reminds me of the rest of the complex. Messy. The first thing I notice is the smell. It reeks of marijuana. The second thing I notice is the clutter. The living room is in disarray. To the left, there's a sofa without any cushions. Right in front of me, there's a bookshelf without any shelves. Next to that, there's a random mattress tilted against the back wall. There are children's toys scattered around the floor.

Michael can clearly see the disgust written on my face. "Sorry for the chaos. We just moved in. Also, my roommate is disgusting," he says.

"How many kids do you have?" I ask.

"You're funny. None. My roommate has a daughter, though," he responds.

We walk past the living room, through the dirty kitchen, and into a hallway. His room is the first on the left.

"I won't bite," he says, sitting on the bed and motioning me to come in.

I look around. There's another room past his to the left, and then the bathroom is all the way at the end on the right. *The living room isn't an option.* I opt to walk into his room, hoping for a safe haven.

It's a small room. Or maybe he just has large furniture, making the room appear to be tiny. Against the wall to the left, there's a tall, wooden dresser with cologne on top of it. Against the wall to right, there's a short, three-shelf bookcase with notebooks piled on each shelf, and a few bags of Doritos and hot Cheetos. *Really bruh, hot Cheetos is what we doing.* There are also three candles burning and some incense lit. A long dresser that comes up to my waist sits next to the bookcase on the left. There's a 60-inch TV on top of the dresser, along with some shoeboxes, trash, papers, a few shirts, a record player, and some more trash.

"Clean much?" I ask, picking up a few crumbled pieces of paper off the dresser, then dropping them on the floor.

"Shut up," he fires back, turning on the TV. "You wanna watch a movie?"

Sure, I'll watch a movie with you, you random stranger. "What ya got?" I ask.

He responds by flipping on his fire stick to show the latest flicks.

Still standing, I push off my shoes and continue to look around the room. DING. My phone goes off, showing a text from Earl asking when I'll be home next. I hit the home button, ignore the text, and continue to look around. Above the tall, wooden dresser, there are pictures of Michael and his mother, the same woman I saw on his Tinder profile. There are also pictures of him with a woman and a man.

"Who are they?" I ask.

"Damn, you nosey," he responds.

"My bad," I say back.

"Come over here, sit down, get comfortable," he motions for me to come sit next to him on the bed. I follow.

"You want some pizza?" he asks.

"Where are you ordering it from?" I ask.

"Your mama's house," he fires back quickly.

I don't have time for this childish shit. I start to stand up, but he grabs my arm and doesn't let me move.

"I'm playin'. We can order from wherever you want. You want some Jet's?" he asks sincerely.

"That's fine. Will you order me a veggie pizza with no black olives, please?" I answer.

"You don't eat meat?" he asks.

"Not the edible kind," I say with a smirk.

"I got something for you," he says.

"I'll pass. Thanks, though," I fire back.

"What do you wanna watch?" he asks, ignoring my comment and rolling his eyes.

After going back and forth on whether to watch a comedy or a horror flick, we decide on one of the Chucky movies. Michael turns off the lights, slides back onto the bed, and taps his chest for me to lie on him. Clearly, I'm out of my mind, because I pull off my hoodie, revealing a tank top, and lie on his chest. He hits the play button and whispers, "I can't believe you actually came."

"That makes two of us," I respond.

The movie is playing, but the only thing I can concentrate on is Michael's right hand moving up and down my back. Every time his hand strokes a little lower, my legs begin to shake, forming a puddle in between my legs. While he's watching the movie, my eyes are closed and I'm dreaming of everything I want.

"What are you thinking about?" he whispers.

Do I answer truthfully or lie? "Everything I wish we were doing instead of watching this movie," I say back coyly.

"What does that mean? Would you rather watch something else?" he asks.

"I don't need a movie to keep me occupied," I say back.

He grabs the remote and hits the pause button: "What were you thinking about when your eyes were closed?"

"You saw that?" I respond with a quiet laugh to myself.

"Of course," he replies. "Are you going to tell me?"

"Every time I close my eyes I see you softly pushing me against a wall, tilting my face up, kissing me. My breathing is slow, my heart is beating out of my chest, and I'm nervous but excited. My eyes are closed and my hands are making their way from your face, to your arms, to your pants.

"You push my hands away. Holding me against the wall, you tease me, kissing from my lips to my neck and down my chest. I try to move you over to the bed, but you're holding me still, unbuttoning my shirt, and sliding my left bra strap down.

"I ask nicely, 'Please?'

"You start to make your way back from my chest, to my neck, to my ear, asking, 'Please what?'

"Instead of answering, I try to move you again. But you're not having it. You say, 'Use your words' with a coy smile. I whisper, 'I need it.' 'What?' you ask back. 'You,' I reply."

Instead of responding, he grabs my face and gives me a deep kiss. We're lying on our sides, he's pulling me in closer with one arm, and I'm holding his face with two hands.

In between kisses, he whispers, "I'm really glad you came."

"Me too," I say back softly, trying to catch my breath.

He pulls back, giving me two more pecks on the mouth, then turns me over so we're both facing the same wall. It's late, he's tired, and I'm tired. "Wanna spend the night?" he whispers.

"Ok, but I have to leave around 4 a.m.," I respond. We're both lying there, still kind of strangers, not comfortable enough with each other to get too relaxed and possibly start snoring.

After five minutes, I sit up. "Um, where's the pizza?" I ask.

"Shit, I knew I forgot to do something," he fires back.

We both laugh, and fall asleep holding hands.

Three

———

I MAKE IT HOME AROUND 4:15 A.M., let Zeus out, and crawl into my own bed.

It's finally Friday.

I walk into work at 7:00 a.m. I have two texts from Earl asking when I'm coming home next, a text from the dog walker asking if he's still on at noon, a text from my mom saying she loves me, and a good morning text from Michael.

I try to turn on the computer, but it's not working. For some reason my computer and phone are both down. I ask my co-worker Denise to call IT for me. Within minutes, the IT guys are at my desk, asking me to move so they can work their magic. I grab my notebook and go find an empty desk to start checking my emails from my phone.

I scan through my emails and find a message from Tim, one of the refinance bankers at my company. Every once in a while, purchase clients will accidentally call the refinance side. The refinance banker is supposed to send them to a different hotline where a purchase banker will answer, but Tim will take a message and send them directly to me. Tim's a super sweet guy. I'd date him if he wasn't a short, hairy, Jewish man who's a borderline alcoholic. I open the email:

Hey Roxie,

There's a client in Michigan that needs a call. I can't remember her name but her number is 713-934-0945. Could you give her a call before 8:00 a.m. Central Time, please?

Thanks,

Tim

The current time is 8:15 a.m. Central Time. "Shit," I mutter to myself.

My computer is down and I don't have any information on this chick, and my work phone is down but I seriously need this deal. In the back of my head, I hear my manager yelling, "Work calls should always be done on work phones!" The government requires all calls about mortgages to be recorded. However, this is a dire emergency. I'm falling behind on my numbers, and I need the deal in order to not get fired.

I feel a faint feeling of despair. Ignoring it, I pick up my cell phone and make the call. I justify the call by telling myself I'll just call the client, figure out who she is, and set an appointment to call her back later.

The phone rings three times. "Hello, this is Maria Washington."

"Hello, Maria. My colleague Tim told me you were looking to purchase a home in New Jersey," I say.

"Sí, sí, I am," she says back with a Spanish accent.

"Fantastic. My name is Roxanne Evans, and I'm a purchase specialist with Excel Loans. We are the second largest online lender in the country, and I am licensed in multiple states, including New Jersey. I've been here for about three years, and I absolutely love it. I also moved here from Michigan, which is awesome," I tell her and then continue explaining to her who I am, how the process with Excel works, and the steps that she'll go through.

"Maria, IT is doing maintenance on the company's system, and everything is down temporarily. Would it be possible to give you a call back within the hour?" I ask.

"I'm actually leaving for work in about 30 minutes and will not be able to talk until tomorrow," she responds.

Nervous about losing another deal, I fire back, "You know what? I'll just take your information down and we'll go from there. How does that sound?"

"Sounds great to me," Maria says.

During the conversation, I discover Maria is looking to buy a three-bedroom home in Houston, Texas. She's 30 years old and works in IT. I keep looking at the clock, thinking she'll want to get off the phone for work, but our quick conversation goes from 30 minutes to two hours with Maria doing a lot of the talking.

Maria graduated from Princeton with a degree in computer science and immediately landed a job in an IT department. She works with the government, breaking into the computers of hackers who are potential terrorists. Right now, she's relocating from Orlando, Florida, to Michigan after catching her husband of eight years cheating. She tells me everything—from how she hacked his cell phone and email accounts to how she read his messages to his mistress. Then she explains how she hacked her husband's mistress's car at a stoplight one day. She stopped the car from moving forward for an entire day. Maria makes sure to clarify that no one was injured; she just thought that stopping the woman's car would stop her from seeing her husband for that day. The longer our conversation goes on, the more Maria starts to spiral into a rage. Just before I think she's about to burst into tears, I bring her back by talking about how great her new home will be.

"Maria, after speaking with you, I'm fairly positive everything will go through our system quickly. Can you send over your pay stubs, bank statements, W2's, mortgage statement, home owners insurance and declaration page? Then I'll have my manger charge your card so we can get everything into processing today," I say, excited to add another deal to my name for the month.

"Sure, why not. How much is it?" she asks.

"It's $400 to get you in processing," I respond.

"Ok," she says, then reads her credit card aloud.

"Maria, give me one second, and I'll have my manager charge the card to get you into processing. We'll charge you the full $400 right now to make sure the card is working," I say.

"You mean to make sure I have $400 in my account," she responds.

I laugh, "May I place you on hold for a moment?"

"Of course, go ahead," she says.

I charge the card through Max's computer. Then, magically, my computer comes back on.

"Hey, Maria, I'm back, and my computer is working again. I see you sent over the purchase agreement, the bank statements, and your pay stubs. Let me get all of this into the system, get your credit report attached to the file, and send you some documents," I say.

"Roxanne, thank you so much. It's been such a pleasure speaking with you. I feel like we're best friends," Maria says.

I laugh, "Yeah, Maria, it's definitely been a great time speaking to you as well. I'll give you a call tomorrow at 8 a.m. Central Time, okay?"

"Okay, love you so much, bye," Maria says, then hands up the phone.

"Denise!" I shout. "Let me tell you about this crazy-ass client I just talked to."

Denise spins around. She sits in the next cubicle over from me. She loves the drama. "You have my attention," Denise says.

"Number one, I just talked to a woman for over two and a half hours straight. Number two, she just told me she pretty much tried to kill her husband's mistress after hacking into his phone and email accounts," I fire back with excitement.

"Um, what? Shouldn't you report that to the police?" she says with a nervous look on her face.

"The problem is I made the call on my cell phone because my work phone was down," I respond.

"ROXANNE, WHAT THE HELL!" Denise shouts. "You're going to get fired if you keep pulling shit like that."

"I know, I know, but I needed the deal and she had to talk at that specific time," I say back, feeling bad.

Denise looks at me and then asks what else happened. I explain that the client is leaving her husband, relocating, and that she works for the government, hacking hackers.

"I don't like working for clients like that," Denise says.

I look at her with a blank face. *This bitch will work with anyone who will give her business.* "Why not?" I ask.

"Because what if this deal goes left? She's going to hack into your life and ruin it," Denise says.

"People aren't that crazy. And she looks great on paper. Nothing can screw this loan up," I fire back.

"Everyone looks good on paper," Denise says while turning back around to her desk.

Denise is an original gangsta in the mortgage game. She's been doing this for 15 years. This is her third mortgage company, and she only writes clean and easy loans. She always tells me she's hit rock bottom before and she's not going back.

An hour goes by, and I have Maria's entire file finished. I shoot it over to Max for him to look over, and then he sends it up to our processors. Our processors then check over the documents to make sure all the numbers are correct. Then they verify everything. They'll call Maria's place of employment to verify with their HR how much she makes and how long she's been there. They'll also hire an appraisal company to go look at the new home. After which, they'll be the new point of contact for the loan.

* * *

SATURDAY COMES AROUND, AND INSTEAD OF GOING TO WORK, I DECIDE TO HANG OUT WITH MICHAEL. He's asked me to dinner and a movie.

DING. DING. DING. I get three text messages back-to-back. It's Maria asking for an update on her loan. Instead of responding, I shut my phone off. It's Saturday, and I'm not doing anything work-related.

Dinner and a movie turn into dinner, a movie, a sleepover, breakfast, Netflix and a chill Sunday, and another sleepover.

Monday morning arrives. I head into work on cloud nine. When I get to my desk, I turn my phone on and have five voicemails and 13 new text messages from Maria, the last one deeply disturbing. *Roxanne, I really thought you were different. I thought you were dependable. I thought you were going to help me out with this loan. I see you're just like the rest of them.*

Shocked, I pick up the phone to call Maria, but her number has been disconnected. I call the processor on the file and ask if she's heard from Maria.

"Roxie, this deal is dead. Those pay stubs Maria sent you were fake," she responds.

"What do you mean they're fake?" I ask.

"I called the government office in Orlando, Florida, and they told me the Maria Washington who worked in IT is deceased," she says.

"Thanks," I respond and hang up the phone. I have no other words.

As soon as the phone hits the receiver, a new email comes in from an unknown email account.

Sender: *Unknown*

Subject: *Hello*

I'm going to ruin you.

That was all it said. "I'm going to ruin you." My face gets warm, and my hands start to sweat.

"MAX!" I shout to my manager. He runs over. "What the fuck is this?" I ask.

He reads the message, "Roxie, forward that to me right now and don't do anything else."

I hit send and back away from the computer.

"Don't worry, Roxie. I'm sure it's an accident or some kind of joke or something. I'm going to send this to IT so we can figure out who sent it. Just keep on working," Max says.

Trying to brush it off, I log back into my phone. For the next few hours, I continue to take call after call of unqualified clients. Some have credit issues, others employment issues, and others are looking for other types of loans and not even trying to purchase a home. Someone is either playing with me or I'm having a terrible day.

"I'm going to grab lunch," I yell out to Max. I have to get out of the office. I need something happy to cheer me up. And, of course, food can fill any void. I take my lunch break and an extra 18 minutes of company time, eating Thai food, stalking every girl who's commented on Earl's Facebook page—*yes, I have a problem*—and staring into the sky.

It's a beautiful day. It's 73 degrees outside, and there's not a cloud in sight. While sitting in the parking lot, I contemplate not going back.

DING. My phone goes off, and it's a text from an unknown sender. *Bitch, you're gonna wish you were dead.*

I run into the building to show Max.

"Roxie!" Max shouts as I walk back into the building. "Can I see you in my office?"

I nod and start heading to my desk to put my things down first, but halfway to my desk, he shouts, "Now!"

People close to the office look up in shock, because it takes a lot to upset Max.

"Max, look at this text message," I say, out of breath.

"Did you have a situation with a client?" he asks.

"A situation?" I ask. "Max, what are you talking about? Look at this text message."

He ignores me. "Client services has been blowing up my phone for the last 30 minutes saying that you committed mortgage fraud," he responds.

"Max, are we talking about Maria Washington here?" I ask.

"Yes, she's called the Better Business Bureau, and she's filed a complaint against you with client relations."

I look at him with no expression.

He continues, "She says you told her she was qualified for a loan and that you checked everything."

"Max, I did check everything. The problem is that she doesn't work where she says she did. Call the processor," I borderline scream at him.

"I've already talked to the processor. The client says you told her that you would help her out and that she could fake her pay stubs and bank statements. Maria says that you called her from your cell phone so that no one from the office would know that you were helping her out," Max says.

"WHAT?" I scream. "I never said that. The only reason I called her from my cell phone is because the computer and phones were down."

"Roxie, you know the policy about calling a client on your cell phone," Max says. "We have recorded lines for a reason."

"Yes, I understand that, but the client needed a call before 8 a.m. Instead of losing a client, I called on my cell phone," I respond.

"I don't care what you did, you made the wrong move. My hands are tied. You're fired," he says, looking down at his hands.

"But this isn't my fault. I would never tell a client that they could change their pay stubs. I didn't do this. I would never do this!" At this point I'm frantically crying and screaming. "Look at this text I got! This Maria person is trying to ruin me! She's trying to ruin my life!"

"Roxie, there's nothing I can do. Security will walk you out of the building," Max says.

"Walk me out of the building? What about my stuff? You're not even going to let me grab my things?" I ask.

"I'm sorry, Roxanne. Goodbye," Max says before getting up to open the door.

That's when two security guards walk in to escort me out of the building.

Four

—

MY ALARM CLOCK GOES OFF AT ITS NORMAL TIME, 5:00 A.M., but instead of jumping up to hit the gym for my daily run, I hit stop on my alarm. Why start my day early when I don't have a job to go to? Thoughts start running through my mind. *Did I make the worst decision of my life making that call? Will anyone ever hire me again? What if I end up back in my mom's basement, living with her and her husband and my grandmother forever?*

I look for my phone. I had thrown it against the wall the night before because it wouldn't stop ringing. Michael wanted to hang out, co-workers were calling to see what happened, and endless social media updates about people's happy lives with their baby announcements, engagement announcements, and new job announcements were pissing me the fuck off.

I find my phone under a shattered picture of my brother and his girlfriend and call Anne Evans.

"Mom," I say.

"Roxie," she responds with her worried voice. "Are you hurt, baby? What's wrong?"

"I got fired. And I'm pretty sure someone is trying to ruin me."

"Ruin you? Roxanne, what are you talking about."

"I don't know, Mom. I tried to help this client, and she ended up lying and saying that I committed mortgage fraud," I respond, explaining the entire situation with tears falling down my face.

"Roxanne, it's time to come home."

"Come home and do what?" I scream. "What about my lease? What about my life here?"

"Roxanne, it's time to come home," she repeats in the same voice.

I look at the phone. Annoyed. Sad. Pissed. Wanting her to just listen and not try to fix the situation.

"Mom, Max is calling me. I'll call you right back. Love you. Bye," I say, hanging up the phone before she can get another word out. Max isn't calling; I just can't talk to her for another moment.

DING. It's another text from Michael. He's been blowing me up since last night. But I haven't had the strength to talk to anyone since being walked out of Excel Loans.

Michael: *Hey. Are you there? Did I do something to piss you off? Are you okay? Call me, I'd love to see you.*

Instead of responding, I log into Facebook and head to Michael's Facebook page. There's a new post. It's a picture of me sleeping the night we met. The caption reads #newbae. I smile, double tap the home button, and look at his text messages.

Me: *Hey babe. I'm really sorry I ghosted you last night. I got fired from my job—long story. Would love to see you tonight. Come over around 7pm. I'll cook dinner and we can watch Star Wars. K?*

Michael: *Can't wait to see you.*

My phone starts buzzing. It's Mom calling again. I hit ignore. Drop my phone and roll back over in bed.

* * *

I MAKE A GROCERY LIST BEFORE HEADING OUT THE DOOR. I plan on making spaghetti with vegan meatballs. I hope Michael will like it because it's my favorite dish and I make it at least once a week. I attempt to remote start my car before heading out, but for some reason it won't start.

Inside the car, I hit the brake pedal and push the button to start the car. But nothing happens. "FUCK!" I shout. This is turning out to be one of the worst weeks ever.

Looking at the list, I really only need a few things—like noodles and tomato sauce. I decide to order an Uber. I have a $100 gift card for Uber from some random raffle that I need to spend before it expires.

* * *

A CAR PULLS UP. "Roxie?" the driver asks.

"That's me," I say.

"I'm Jake, and I'll be your Uber driver. I noticed we're going to Kroger. Are you heading to work?" he asks.

"Nope, I'm just heading there to grab a few things," I say, looking at him through the mirror. Jake's an older gentleman—probably 60 or 70 years old. Gray hair. Super skinny. Driving with his hands on the wheel at the ten and the two.

"Well, ma'am, I don't mind waiting for you and bringing you back home. All you have to do is send another request. I'll respond and wait in the same spot I drop you off," he says.

"That would be awesome, thank you so much," I respond.

We arrive in less than seven minutes. I really probably could have walked to Kroger. "I'll put in the new request, and I'll be right back," I say.

I run in and grab a few items, then head to the self-checkout line. It's really amazing how people can go through life now without speaking to another human being. Technology is insane. I ring up my items and go to pay, but my card is rejected.

"Ma'am, your card was declined," the store clerk says aloud in front of everyone.

NO FUCKING SHIT. "I'll try again," I respond.

"Knock yourself out," she says, walking over to my station. But my card is rejected for the second time.

"You can try up here," she says, motioning for me to head up to her station.

"Okay, thanks so much," I say, handing her my card.

"Nope, this card isn't working. Would you like to try another one?" she asks.

"No, I'm sorry," I respond, then quickly walk out of the store. I have a cold sweat, but my face is burning hot from embarrassment. I know I have money in my account. I can't be broke yet. *What the hell have I been spending my money on?*

I jump back into the Uber driver's car and ask him to take me home. "Where's your groceries?" he asks. "I accidently forgot my wallet at the apartment," I lie through my teeth to avoid feeling the humiliation of having had a rejected card all over again.

"Oh, I'll just take you home and bring you right back," he says sweetly.

"No, it's okay. If you take me home, I'll just order pizza. I don't have time to cook anymore, unfortunately," I lie, because it's easier than telling the truth.

My face is still hot from embarrassment. In the back of the car, I open up my Chase account and see that all my accounts have $0 balances. Instead of freaking out in the back of the Uber, I patiently wait the seven minutes it takes to drive back so that I can freak the fuck out at home. "Thanks so much. Have a great night," I say while waving and jumping out of the car.

I run into my apartment. It's a flat on the nice side of town. I pay $1,850 a month, so it better be nice. I have two bedrooms, a giant living room, and a beautiful kitchen area where the window looks out at the river and New York City.

I call Chase immediately, pressing "0" a million times instead of listening to the prompts.

"Hello, this is Bridget with Chase, how may I assist you today?" a pleasantly voiced woman says over the phone.

"Bridget, my name is Roxanne Evans, and all my money has been taken out of my accounts!" I bellow.

"I'm so sorry that this happened to you, Roxanne. Do you mind if I get the last four of your social to verify your account?"

I punch a wall. "9870," I say back.

"Thank you. I'll also need you to verify your address."

"1740 Riverwood Drive. Apartment 5C. North Bergen, New Jersey."

"Thank you very much, Roxanne. So you'd like to report that your money was stolen?"

"Yes, Bridget, my money was stolen out of my account."

"Roxanne, it appears there was a large withdrawal of $12,340.52 yesterday at a bank in North Bergen, New Jersey. Did you make that withdrawal?"

"NO!" I scream, "I did not make that withdrawal! Otherwise I wouldn't be calling you."

"Okay, Roxanne. Please hold one minute while I file this claim."

The hold music begins, and she puts me on hold for what seems like an eternity.

"Roxanne, are you still there?"

"Yes, I'm here."

"Okay, I filed a claim stating that $12,340.52 was withdrawn from your account, but you did not make the withdrawal. Within the next few days Chase will put the money back into your account while an investigation is done into what happened. I'll also be sending you a new debit and credit card and changing your accounts. Those cards will arrive within two days," Bridget tells me and continues to explain everything that will happen next.

"Okay, thank you."

"Okay, is there anything else I can do to help you today?"

"No, thank you."

"Well thank you for being the best part of Chase. I hope you have a great day, okay?"

I hang up the phone. Speechless.

* * *

THE DOORBELL RINGS. I look down at my watch and it's already 7 p.m. I look through the peephole and it's Michael.

"Hi, baby," I say, giving him a kiss and fighting back tears. "I'm sorry but we're going to have to order pizza. Something is wrong with my bank account. All my accounts are empty." I thought the words would flow out of my mouth sarcastically, but I'm really five seconds from having a meltdown.

"What?" he asks in disbelief.

"My life is just blowing up right now," I say as tears start running down my face. He puts his arms around me and holds me tight.

"Well, good thing is, I stalked your Instagram and brought your favorite movie so you don't have to suffer through another Star Wars film," he tells me as he pulls out a *Just Wright* DVD from behind his back.

"How are you so perfect?" I say, grabbing his face, giving him a wet kiss from my tears.

Michael takes it a step further, grabbing my face and sliding his tongue to the back of my throat, moving his hands down to my waist. He pushes me backwards, through the doorway, to my bedroom. Still kissing me, he slides off his shoes and starts unbuttoning my shirt.

"Is this okay?" he asks innocently. I reach up for more kisses, whip off his belt, and slide down his pants.

I push him backwards onto the bed and open the hole in his boxers, pulling his dick out. Kneeling in between his legs, I give it a kiss. I then put my mouth around the tip of his dick. I twirl my tongue around and then deep throat his penis. He's gripping the bedspread, and I'm going up and down, switching between sucking and kissing his dick. Michael lifts me up by my underarms and throws me on the bed. Completely surprised by his strength, I push myself back on the bed, trying to regain my composure. He pulls off my jeans, then my thong, and tries to climb on the bed.

I put my foot on his shoulder, stopping him. "Boxers off," I demand.

They hit the floor.

Michael kisses up my thighs, to my clit, to my stomach, then my neck. I grab his dick and put it in. He makes love to me, giving me slow and deep pumps until we both cum.

* * *

"SO WHAT HAPPENED WITH YOUR JOB?" Michael asks.

I tell him the entire situation. Starting with my crazy-ass client. I don't stop there and continue on my rant, telling him about everything that has happened today as well.

"Wait," Michael says about the client. "What did she say she did?"

"She said she was some crazy hacker who looks for terrorists or some shit. Who really knows? I have no idea who I was talking to."

"Roxie, I think this is my fault," he says sitting up in the bed.

"What the hell are you talking about?" I ask, jumping out of the bed.

"Sit down, please."

"FUCK NO! MICHAEL, WHY WOULD THIS BE YOUR FAULT?" I scream. In my head, I'm trying to figure out how I went from zero to 10 so quick.

"Sit down, and I'll tell you."

I sit down on the bed in the corner farthest from him. The distance is really for his protection, because I'm trying not to punch him in the face.

"Okay. This has happened to women I've dated before. Never this extreme, but they start dating me, and bad things start happening."

"What the fuck do you mean bad things start happening?" I ask, now feeling that my anger is fair.

"The last woman I dated had her bank accounts mysteriously drained. And the woman before started having car troubles whenever we had plans. It was as if her battery died, but when technicians came out to look at the car it was fine. The technology had been hacked."

"Michael, you're not making any sense."

"Please let me finish," he says. "Two years ago, I broke it off with a woman named Angela. She's a computer hacker who works for the government. She has the ability to manipulate any type of technology that she wants to."

"WHAT?" I scream, all the blood rushing to my head.

"Please let me finish," he pauses. "Angela and I dated for six years; we were engaged to get married. Then I walked away."

"You were engaged."

"Roxie."

"Okay, keep going."

"During the last year of our relationship, Angela started changing. She started becoming very aggressive and controlling. She wanted to know where I was all the time and who I was talking to. Every time my phone went off, she was asking me who was texting me. Every time my phone rang, she was looking at it trying to see who was calling. She had nothing to worry about—I'd never do anything like cheat on someone—but it all became too much."

"Okay, so what happened?"

"I caught her hacking my phone calls, text messages, and emails. She was recording all of my calls and playing them back and reading through my texts and email accounts."

"What the fuck?"

"I told her that enough was enough and that I wanted to end things with her. Then she started to spiral. First she'd show up at my door at all hours of the night. She'd blow my phone up, even if I changed my number or blocked her. She'd send me emails and texts from unknown numbers and unknown accounts. She even called my mother and told her if I didn't get back with her, she'd ruin my life."

"That's fucking crazy, Michael."

"We lived in Michigan at the time. I moved here to escape her."

"Wait, Michigan," I snap. "You never told me you lived in Michigan."

"Yeah, I grew up there. Crazy story is I think we knew each other when we were kids when—"

I cut him off. I don't give a fuck about a stupid story from when we were kids. "Escape her? That makes her sound like a crazy person," I say through clenched teeth.

Michael ignores that and blows past his story. "I didn't date for over a year after that. I randomly got on Tinder a few months ago because a friend suggested it. The first two women I met on the site weren't my type. I mean, we talked for a few days, went on a few dates, then things were over."

"Then why do you think it was Angela that was messing with them?"

"I didn't suspect it was her until now. It's insane that a client called you, telling that crazy story, then your car won't start, and your bank accounts are drained. This is more than a coincidence."

"Fuck, fuck, fuck, fuck, fuck," I start repeating.

"Don't worry. I'm going to fix this," he says.

"How the hell are you going to fix this, Michael? Your crazy ex-fiancé is trying to ruin my life. Look at these texts."

Unknown sender: *Bitch, you're gonna wish you were dead.*

Unknown sender: *I really thought you were different. I see you're just like the rest of them.*

Unknown sender: *You won't be collecting $200 cause you're not passing go, bitch.*

Michael throws the phone to the other side of the room, "Roxie, I promise nothing will happen to you. I'll keep you safe. I'm going to take care of this!"

I want to ask Michael to leave, but I also don't want to be alone, knowing a crazy person is out there plotting to ruin my life. Thinking back, life would have been so much easier traveling back and forth to Michigan to see Earl instead of jumping on Tinder to find love.

Five

—

MICHAEL SHAKES ME AWAKE. "Are you in a relationship?" he asks.

I don't respond, still trying to open my eyes. "Roxie, are you in a relationship with a man named Earl?" he asks again.

"First of all, it's four in the morning. Second of all, I'm not in a relationship. Otherwise, I wouldn't have slept with you last night," I respond.

Michaels puts his phone in my face. Once my eyes can finally focus, I grab the phone. There are half-naked pictures of me on Earl's Instagram account.

"What the fuck is this?" I shout, reading the caption: "My Number 1."

"I should be asking the same thing," Michaels mutters under his breath.

I grab my phone off the nightstand and call Earl, but his phone is disconnected. I have six missed calls from my brother Ricky, 21 text messages in a group chat with my best friends, and one message from an unknown sender.

Unknown sender: *"Nice tits, bitch."*

I turn the phone around and show Michael. "This shit is getting ridiculous," I say. "Naked pictures on Instagram is taking it a little far. I don't see why she's targeting me and not you. I feel like there's something you're not telling me."

"By targeting you, she is affecting me, Roxie," he responds.

I jump up, rolling my eyes. "I'm going to the fucking cops. I'm not dealing with this shit anymore," I tell him.

"I'm going with you," he says.

"Don't you have work?" I fire back.

"Can't you wait for me?" he asks.

"No!" I fire back in the meanest voice possible.

* * *

AFTER WAITING 90 MINUTES, AN INVESTIGATOR WILL FINALLY SEE ME.

"How can I help you?"

"I'm being harassed by my boyfriend's ex-fiancé."

"Harassed how?"

"First she targeted me at work, getting me fired. She's ruined my car and drained my bank accounts."

"How did she get you fired?" he asks.

I explain the entire story about how Angela called under a false pretense, sent in fake documents, then lied and said I told her to do it.

"Okay, and what proof do you have?"

"Proof? What kind of proof do you want?" I ask.

"Do you have a recorded call so that we can tell that it's her?"

"No."

"Okay, what do you have?"

"I don't have anything."

"Okay, well, tell me what else happened."

"Don't you need to be writing this down?" I ask.

"Just continue," he says.

"Well she hacked into the technology in my car and broke it. Then she drained all my bank accounts."

"Again, ma'am, what proof do you have?"

"'My boyfriend can tell you how crazy she is. It's her. She's messing with me."

"Ma'am, unfortunately, until you have some proof, there's nothing we can do. I have nothing to put in a report."

"Can't you go talk to her? Call her? Tell her to leave me alone?"

"Ma'am, I'm going to have to ask you to leave. Why don't you two sit down and squash it yourselves," he suggests.

Realizing he's not going to help me, I stand up and walk out of the police station. I'm going to have to handle this myself. Before getting in the rental car, I fire off a message . . .

Look you stupid bitch. You've now ruined my career, you stole all my money, you broke my car, you're posting naked pictures of me online, and for what? You're upset Michael left you? What the hell is it that you want?

I hit send, unlock the doors, jump in the car, and that's all that I remember.

* * *

Angela

I BET I SOUND CRAZY TO YOU GUYS. I'm trying to ruin someone else's life over a man. But listen to my side before you cast judgment.

Michael and I met when we were seven years old. We took ballet class together. Our parents raised us to be best friends. We started dating at Princeton, graduated together summa cum laude, and planned a life together.

My entire world circled around Michael. Then one day I wake up to a note that read, "We should take a break." Three days later, all his stuff is gone, he's moved to New Jersey, and he's no longer taking my calls. Then the cherry on top—he's wiped out OUR bank accounts and taken the Range Rover I bought him, leaving me carless.

To say this pissed me off is an understatement. At the time I was working for the F.B.I. as a hacker. It was my job to find terrorists recruiting people online, shut down their sites, and reverse their damage.

I was great at my job until Michael left me. I got fired after my manager caught me tracking Michael's location. HE WOULDN'T ANSWER MY CALLS. I just wanted to know where he was, who he was talking to, and what he was doing.

In one week, I lost my fiancé, my job, my money, and my car. And to make matters worse, I was pregnant.

Fast-forward to today: I'm working at Best Buy because I can't get a job anywhere else. I have a two-year-old. I live in a tiny shit apartment, and I'm single because no man wants to date a woman with a baby.

Last week, I'm surfing the web under my fake name, Maria Washington, when I see Michael has a new post on his Facebook. It's a picture of that bitch Roxanne Evans. Roxie may not remember me, but I remember her. All three of us grew up dancing at Legacy Dance Studio back in the day. Michael's been pining after her since we were seven years old. Seeing that post sent me into a rage. I now realize she's the real reason he left me. They've probably been talking to each other in secret for years and plotting against me. I'm going to ruin both of them.

* * *

"HELLO!" Roxie shouts.

She wakes up with her arms tied behind her back and her feet tied to a chair, in the dark. Angela had grabbed her at the police station and taken her to an abandoned building.

"Is anyone out there?" Roxie screams.

Six

—

ROXIE'S PHONE RINGS.

Michael: "Roxie, where the hell are you? I've been calling you all day."

Angela: "Awww, are you looking for your little girlfriend?"

Michael: "Angela?"

Angela: "Oooohhhh, now you remember me?"

Michael: "Where's Roxie?"

Angela: "111 Jefferson Street Hoboken, New Jersey. Come alone."

Click. The phone hangs up.

* * *

I OPEN MY EYES AND TRY TO FOCUS. There's a dim light shining above my head. My hands are duct-taped together in my lap, and my feet are taped together. There's also a rope cutting off my circulation and trapping me to the chair.

The first thing I notice is a rancid smell exuding from somewhere. It reeks of mildew and rat feces. I'm in someone's unfinished basement. The chair I'm in is stuck in the middle of the room facing what I would guess is the back wall. There are boxes lined against the wall right in front of me. I notice peeling white wallpaper and holes in the wall. It looks like someone might have used the wall as a punching bag.

The floor is cement. I'm missing my left shoe, and the cold floor is freezing the balls of my feet. I try to turn to my left and right, but the rope around my chest is so tight I can barely move. *If I can move the rope above my big-ass titties, I think I'd be able to escape.* Out of the corner of my eye, I can see a dirty, smeared sheet covering a green couch in the corner. There's some broken glass and old portraits lying on the floor in front of it. I vaguely remember knocking the pictures over while being dragged down the stairs. I'm guessing the path to freedom is the stairway behind me.

I had worn some jeans and a Michigan hoodie to the police station with my orange Converse shoes. Now, looking down, I see that I'm wearing some gray sweatpants and a black sweatshirt. *Did this bitch change me?* The left sleeve of the sweatshirt is ripped near my bicep. I remember struggling when I was going in and out of consciousness. Also, there's either dried sweat, spit, or blood on the right side of my face. It reminds me of dry Halloween paint. When I squint my face, I can feel it crack. It's freezing to the point that I can see my breath. Another thing—I swear I hear cartoons and laughing echoing from upstairs.

Think, Roxie. Think. How are you going to make it out of this trap of doom? First, I need to somehow get my hands and feet free because I don't think anyone is coming to save me.

* * *

Michael

I'M NOT PERFECT. But I'm not a bad guy. Angela started off as such a sweet girl. We fell in love almost instantly. When I met her, she was a short, feisty ball of fire. She stands about 5'3", but she has an intense fire about her. She has long, wavy hair, and she's a mix of black and Puerto Rican.

Our relationship started off with us texting all day and going on dates every night. Then we moved in together after three months of romance. We both met each other's families, and we thought we'd spend the rest of our lives together. We were in our young twenties— just out of college. We were both Princeton graduates, so we had no problem landing great jobs. We were employed, made more money than we needed, and had nearly zero responsibilities.

Over the years we fought about little stuff: me not putting the seat down, us not having enough time for each other, and the apartment being a disaster. However, we never fought over anything I thought would tear us apart until I quit my day job in an office and opened my own HVAC business. I started Forrester's Heating & Cooling, L.L.C., in Michigan and later moved it to New Jersey. I started the company with my best friend, Ed. We handle heating, ventilation, and air conditioning. At Princeton, I studied business, so I knew how to handle the business side. Ed grew up working in HVAC, so he knew the ins and outs of the organization.

In order to grow our business, we did any job. By any job, I mean ANY job—no matter how big or small it was. Angela didn't like that I was getting calls at all times of the day and night. She started to grow jealous of the women calling my phone and adding me on social media. I would have never cheated on her, but the new attention I was getting was too much for her.

Angela started listening to my phone calls and going through my texts. If it was a woman, she'd call her back and tell her my company didn't have time to do the job. Word started getting out that we were turning clients away, and she started to ruin my business. I tried to have countless talks with her. I talked to her parents about it. I involved her friends in the situation. She pushed all of us away because she was convinced I was cheating on her. Lastly, I contacted a therapist so we could go to couples therapy. I was in love with Angela, and I wanted to spend the rest of my life with her, but we needed to get back on the same page.

Angela never showed up at the agreed-upon time, but the therapist and I agreed that I could see her for one-on-one treatment. Through my weekly sessions—which lasted almost a year—I learned to love myself, and to see how toxic my relationship with Angela really was. In the end, this awakening gave me the strength to leave her and end all communication with her.

During that year I spent in therapy, I did my best to work with Angela and fix the situation. She never gave an inch, and, finally, I decided to leave. I broke things off with Angela, packed up all my stuff, and convinced Ed to make the journey to New Jersey. I blocked her number and her email, and didn't tell her where I was going.

Ed and I had to pick up and completely restart our business. It was tough, but two years later, our company is still standing.

Fast-forward to now. With Angela kidnapping Roxie, I know I have to get involved. I'm the only person who can talk her off a ledge. I throw on a jacket, grab my keys, and make the trek to Hoboken.

Following my GPS, I twist and wind through a dark neighborhood. One hundred eleven Jefferson Street is at the end of a subdivision. The house is an old Victorian manor, standing alone on a hill. It is dingy, paint-flaked, and seriously neglected. The windowpanes are smeared with age and dirt, and the brickwork is crumbling away. The path to the front door is overgrown with bushes and weeds—the thorns on both reaching out to capture newcomers.

I pull in, turn the car off, and make my way to the front door. I cringe at each creak on the old warped stairs, but it doesn't sway my determination to make it to Roxie. I raise my hand to knock, and a shadow flickers out of the corner of my vision. I freeze, and as I stand there, I catch a scent of Roxie's perfume lingering in the air. A shiver curls through the hairs on the back of my neck as I try to decide what to do next.

I open the door and BAM!

Seven

———

I'M STILL STUCK IN THE BASEMENT TRYING TO FREE MYSELF. I'm attempting to remember everything I learned right before my semester abroad in Europe. I had to do an entire training on responding and defending myself in times of threatening situations. They even taught us how to escape when you're tied up in case you're kidnapped or in a home invasion, a skill it now looked like I was going to have to try to recall and put to use.

I hear a loud thud from the floor above me. I hope Angela had a stroke and died. The stupid bitch.

Focus, Roxie. Focus. I start going through every survival tip I can remember. First, I'll need to shimmy the rope over my boobs so I can raise my arms above my head and then swing them down to break the tape. According to Miguel, my survival class teacher, this maneuver applies stress to the tape and causes it to break.

I start by trying to wiggle myself left and right to get the rope to move. It isn't budging. I try forcing it up by lifting my elbows to the ceiling, but that's not working either. Frustrated, I start moving my body, flailing my trapped arms around and using my legs for momentum.

Then. Plop.

"Shit," I shout from the floor. The chair and I have fallen over during my chaotic attempt to escape. Out of nowhere, the tears burst forth like water from a dam, spilling down the left side of my face to the cold cement. I feel the muscles of my face tremble. An invariable wave shifts through my body, the side effect of the fear of the unknown.

"Stop it, Roxie," I say to myself to convince me to get my shit together.

I take a deep breath and realize the tightness in my chest is gone. Between rocking myself back and forth on the ground and crying hysterically, I must have loosened the rope around my chest. I shimmy my body left and right, moving the rope above my chest. I then use my thumbs to raise the rope over the chair and above my head.

While removing the rope, my body falls away from the chair. Now I'm flopping around on the floor like a fish out of water. I flip on my back, raise my hands above my head, and slam them down, releasing the tape from my arms. Next, I remove the tape from my legs, and, suddenly, I'm free.

My first reaction is to look around for a weapon. Of course, there's nothing around but a few boxes and portraits. While looking around, I hear footsteps. I creep up the stairs without making a sound. It's a narrow staircase with cobwebs hanging down from the ceiling. The steps are carpeted, and there's a wooden rail. I don't dare touch it, as there's a chance it might make a sound. *If this bitch is coming to get me, I'm going to get her first.* However, the footsteps continue past the door.

"It's time to wake up, my love," I hear Angela say through the door. Confused as to who she's talking to, I try to look underneath the door. There's a crack separating the door from the floor. I see a light from an open room to the left. My guess is that it's the kitchen area.

There's an open doorway and what appears to be an island sitting in the middle of the room. The island is blocking me from seeing Angela and who she is talking to.

She repeats, "It's time to wake up, love of my life."

"Angela," Michael responds. His voice seems just as confused as I am. "Angela, what the fuck are you doing?" he asks angrily. "Why am I tied up, and why are you wearing Roxie's clothes?"

"We're together again, baby," Angela says in a sweet voice. "I came back to save you from that whore you were dating. Now we can be a family."

"A family—," Michael starts talking, but Angela cuts him off. "Sabrina, hunny, come here," Angela says loudly.

I hear little feet pattering down the steps. Then I watch tiny feet walk past the door. "Yes, Mommy," a little girl responds.

Now I'm confused as fuck. I had specifically asked Michael if he had any kids and he had told me no. Now I'm listening to a conversation between him, the bitch who kidnapped me, and a little girl who seems to be their child . *What the fuck is next?*

"Meet your Daddy, Sabrina," Angela says.

The room goes silent. It feels like an eternity goes by before anyone says anything.

"Michael, this is your daughter, Sabrina. Don't you have anything to say?" Angela asks.

"Hello, Sabrina, it's a pleasure meeting you. Do you think you can give me and your mom some private time to talk?" Michael asks in the calmest voice possible.

Before I know it, I see the little girl's feet running past the door. Then I hear her making her way back up the stairs.

"Angela, are you out of your fucking mind? We don't have a fucking kid together. Unfucking tie me, right fucking now," Michael says.

BBBBZZZZZZZ.

"OUCH, THE FUCK ANGELA?!" he screams.

"When boys are bad they get tazed," Angela giggles. "We do have a child together, silly. You just saw her."

"Angela, we haven't been together in years. I'd know if we had a kid together," Michael responds.

"It's been exactly two years, Michael. Sabrina is almost two years old. I found out I was pregnant with her right after you left. You know—when you stopped taking my calls and emails," Angela responds.

"But that's beside the point. It's time for you to make a choice, Michael," Angela continues. "You can choose your family or you can choose to rot and die with your whore Roxie. CHOOSE."

I know this is selfish, but the only thing I'm thinking of is myself. *How the hell did I go from falling in love with Earl—who didn't love me back—to falling in love with a man with a crazy baby mama?* This can't be real life. Plus, now she's saying I'm going to rot and die. At that moment, I know it is time to stop snooping and get the fuck on.

I reach to turn the handle of the door, and to my surprise it's unlocked. *Damn, this bitch is dumb as fuck.* I slowly turn the handle, slowly open the door inch by inch, and slide my way out to freedom. I could make a beeline to the door and run. However, my conscience won't let me leave Michael there with the crazy.

It's nighttime, so the house is dark. The only light is coming from the kitchen to my left. Michael and Angela are still talking, but I'm trying to find the best way to Michael followed by how to get the hell out of there. I reach out to touch the wall, which guides me to the right. Across from the basement door, there's a bathroom. If you keep going to the right, there's an opening to a room that looks like a living room. When you walk through the living room, it takes you through a circle to the kitchen. I sneak into the living room, bumping my leg on a couch.

"Sabrina, is that you?" Angela asks. I hear footsteps coming towards me.

"Yes, Mommy," Sabrina's little voice rings from upstairs.

"I'm going to check on our angel, baby. Be right back. Don't move," Angela says. She then kisses Michael on the cheek and makes her way upstairs.

As soon as the coast is clear, I creep into the kitchen. It's a small cook's room. When I walk in, there's a glass table with four orange place settings. There's a sink, refrigerator, oven, and island in the middle of the room. Michael is trapped at the head of the table facing away from my direction. His hands are duct-taped behind his back, and his legs are taped to the chair.

I sneak up behind him and cover his mouth so he doesn't say anything. He's startled, but then looks relieved to see me. I start untying his hands. "We're going to get out of here. Where are your keys?" I whisper.

"I'm so sorry about all of this," he whispers back.

"Michael, where the fuck are your keys?" I respond.

"I don't know," he responds in a somber tone.

Within ninety seconds, he's free from the tape, and we're making our way back through the living room to the front door.

"The front door is right on the other side of this opening. I'll open the door and we'll make a run for it," I whisper. We creep through the living room, holding the wall to find our way. You can see everything from the front door. When you walk in the house, to the left there's a stairway that heads upstairs. If you look straight ahead, there's a narrow hallway that leads to the kitchen. Before you enter the kitchen, there's a door to the left that leads to the basement and a door to the right that leads to a bathroom. Lastly, from the doorway view, there's a living room to the right.

"You ready?" I turn and ask Michael. He nods, and I open the front door that will lead to our freedom.

Angela is standing outside on the doorstep . "How could you do this to us, Michael? Why would you choose her over me, Michael?" Angela screams.

I slam the door and lock it.

"How the fuck did she sneak past us? How did she get outside? Did you hear her? Forget it, find a phone and call the fucking cops," I scream to Michael. We both run in different directions.

I run upstairs, and Michael runs to the kitchen, turning on lights and looking for a phone. "Any luck?" I scream from a room that looks like Sabrina's.

"No!" Michael responds.

There's a twin-size bed with pink bedding, a tiny desk, and a flat screen TV in the room I just ran into. Outfits are scattered around the floor as if someone has been looking for the perfect outfit. There are multiple plates stacked on the desk. I'd guess Angela and Sabrina have been staying there for a few weeks, which makes me wonder how long Angela has been watching me.

"Roxie, where are you?" Michael screams.

"Upstairs," I respond before all the lights go out.

"MICHAEL!" Angela screams from outside the house, "Sabrina and I forgive you! Come out now and we can be a family!"

As I am standing in shock, trying to figure out how I got here, Michael grabs me in the dark. "Roxie," Michael says.

I'm pissed I'm in this situation because of him but also excited he found me in the dark. I wrap my arms around him, asking, "How are we going to get out of this?"

We stand together for a few moments before we hear a noise from downstairs. The front door opens and shuts, its creaking noise bringing a chill to my spine. It sounds like some dying animal, crying out in pain with its last breath. All I know is Angela's now somewhere in the house, and we need to find a way out.

Eight

___

"WE NEED TO GET OUT OF HERE," I WHISPER TO MICHAEL.

"Let's sneak downstairs and out the back door and just make a run for it," Michael says.

"Okay, you grab the door," I respond.

As soon as Michael goes for the door, I feel a breeze hit my face. The door is kicked in and now Angela is staring at us. "Miss me, bitches?" she shouts, holding a gun pointed right at my face. "I tried to be nice, but now I see I'm going to have to kill your little girlfriend to get you to come home to your family," Angela says.

"You're fucking crazy!" I scream.

Angela's phone starts ringing. She looks down at her Apple Watch and rejects the call.

"Put the gun down, Angela!" Michael shouts.

"I'll put it down after I blow her brains out," Angela responds.

"How about I just leave?" I say coyly, putting my hands up and taking a step towards the door.

BANG. Angela fires off a shot from her gun at one of Sabrina's windows. "You're not fucking going anywhere, Peaches," Angela says in a calm voice with her head tilted to the side. Angela's phone continues to ring, and she continues to send it to voicemail.

"Do you need to get that? We can just go while you answer that," I taunt.

Angela glares at me with a death stare.

"Seriously, Ang, this has gone far enough," Michael says.

"Seriously, Ang, this has gone far enough. Wah wah wah," Angela mocks him in a whiny voice. "You know nothing, Michael. You're out here catering to this bitch, hanging out with her, buying her shit, posting pictures of her, and calling her your new bae. I came here to save you. Do you know she has no job, no money, and no car? She's a bottom bitch. She just wants to use you. Don't you understand, Michael?" Angela cries.

"I only lost my job because of your stupid games! I'll get a new job and my money will be replaced. But you—you'll always be a simple, lonely hag. Don't worry, though. I'll raise your daughter to grow up with sense after the cops cart you away!" I scream with frustration.

That is the icing on the cake. Angela charges at me, hitting me in the face with the back of the gun. Angela recovers quickly, steps back, and draws the gun up, now slowly swinging it back and forth between both Michael and me. "You're gonna die tonight," Angela says, looking into my eyes.

DING. DING. Angela looks down at her Apple Watch after two texts come through. She picks up her phone and makes a call.

"Are you okay?" Michael asks, looking over at Roxie.

"Don't talk to me," I respond through clinched teeth as Angela begins going back and forth with someone over the phone.

"That's not a good idea."

Pause.

"I don't want to, bro."

Pause.

"No."

Pause.

"I'm never going to get my way. I don't want that."

Pause.

"Bro, please, no," Angela says.

Pause.

"Ok, whatever, bro. I'll let you handle it."

Angela looks at us, lowers the gun, and reaches into her pocket. She pulls out Michael's keys and throws them to him. A tear rolls down her cheek as she says, "You guys are free to go." She walks into a room across the hall, slams the door, and locks it.

As soon as the door slams, I make a run for the staircase. Michael follows. They run out the front door and to Michael's purple Dodge Charger. Michael beeps the remote to unlock the car and slides into the driver's seat while I run around to get in the passenger side.

"Let's fucking go before that bitch changes her mind," I say without looking his way.

"You don't think that was strange how she just decided to let us go?" Michael asks. "What about my daughter?"

"Bruh, if you want to wait around, go for it. Give me the keys, and you can get your car from my house," I snap back.

"Fuck it," Michael throws the car in drive and speeds away.

It's a silent and long drive home to North Bergen. At the gate to my apartment, Michael brings the car to a stop. "I'm really sorry about everything that happened tonight," Michael says softly.

"Yup, me too," I say holding back tears of frustration not sadness. "Can you just take me home?"

Michael pulls in front of the apartment and tries to lean in to give me a hug. I pretend not to notice and go straight for the door to open it.

"Can I come in?" Michael asks.

"How about I just see you another time?" I respond, slamming the door closed.

Walking up to the door, I see a shadow at my door. I pause and turn back and look at Michael. Our eyes meet. Michael starts getting out of the car. I look back at the door. Out of the shadows steps Earl. A rush of relief runs through my body. I immediately run to him and jump in his arms. He smells the same—like coconuts and palm trees. He's dressed in an all-black jumpsuit with black sneakers.

"Rox, are you okay? I've been blowing up your phone for two days, girl," Earl says. "I swear I didn't put those naked pictures up on social media."

I hold him tighter, hearing Michael swerve off behind me.

"What is going on?" Earl asks. "Your clothes are ripped and your mouth is bleeding. Did he hurt you? I'll kill him."

"No, no, no, babe. I'm okay. Let's go inside where I can explain," I finally respond letting go of him.

I uncover a hidden key under a rock in front of the house. "Did you lose your keys?" Earl asks.

"I think I lost my mind," I respond, opening the door for us to go in. "You want something to drink or eat? I'm going to make some tea," I say in a stale voice.

"Rox, you look like you've been beat up and dragged down the street. As your oldest friend, how about you let me take care of you for once," Earl says. "I promise I can boil some water for some tea. Why don't you wash up and change?" I nod in relief, heading into another room to do just that.

Earl starts making the tea while I stare at my reflection in the mirror. I do not recognize the woman staring back at me. *I can't believe this night. I can't believe any of this happened. I can't believe this bitch hit me.*

I poke my head out the door: "Before I jump in the shower I just wanted to say thank you for being here." Earl looks up from his text and smiles.

"Who you texting?" I ask in a prying way.

"My sister," Earl responds.

I take a few steps forward. "Your long-lost sister? Oh my gosh, that's crazy! I thought you had no idea where she was or what she was doing?" I ask.

"Yeah, she found me two years ago when she found out she was having a baby girl. She needed some help raising her," Earl says.

"Wow, that must have been so great meeting up with her and talking to her again. I'm so happy for you, babe," I say with a smile.

"It's definitely wild. She's introduced me to a different world. I love her, and I'd do anything for her," Earl says.

"I love hearing that," I respond, taking a few steps backward. "I'm gonna hop in the shower real quick. Then I want to hear all about her and your niece," I add before heading back into the room.

I take a quick shower. Clean up the blood on my face. Throw on some comfortable pajamas and socks and heads back out to the living room where Earl is waiting on the couch with an ice pack and some warm tea.

"You're perfect, you know that?" I ask, giving him a kiss on the cheek. "What's your sister's name, by the way?"

The adorably cute accommodating smile from Earl's face washes away. A mean, almost sadistic, expression replaces it. A cold chill runs through the room, and I start to feel a weird vibe.

"Angela," Earl responds with a straight face.

To be continued . . .